C000258688

The Train Ride

Copyright © Nick Voro 2024

First Edition

The Train Ride

VoroBooks, Etobicoke, Ontario, Canada

ISBN: 978-1-7383199-0-9

Typesetting and additional design by Lee Thompson Editing+

To contact the author: Nick_Voro@hotmail.com

THE TRAIN RIDE

T HE TRAIN DELAYED, THE STATION teemed with clustered chattering complaining individuals under one roof standing, sitting and pacing impatiently, including insolent businessmen swinging their freshly-polished leather briefcases, blue-collar workers inconvenienced by their over-packed battered valises, and women ranging from professionals to mothers-to-be clutching purses nervously, perhaps as a preventative measure against pillaging by the tricksters and charlatans also gathered there. Those types were also surrounded by the infirm, some wounded and damaged from the war effort, others with tired and defeated spirits and the sadly permanently damaged, mentally defective, heading for the sanatoriums. There one could also find the rising movers and shakers of the business world, missionaries spreading Christianity and the word of God, diplomatic emissaries and emaciated and travel-weary emigres heading to greener pastures. Many resolutely stared ahead. Not all could fit under the station roof and hide from the stifling sun. But they all stood together as a cohesive unit, perspiring terribly in their togetherness on this especially hot windless day.

Nicholas Price was growing slightly impatient himself, checking his wristwatch every so often. Aside from the delayed train and the sweltering sun, a third annoyance had presented itself, in the form of a man partly hidden behind a raised newspaper, one who was clearly observing him.

4

The looks given were almost imperceptible, completely opposite of incessant. They glided over him, never lingering long enough to become undesirable. The observer did not amateurishly lower the paper excessively or peer over it completely. No, this was someone who knew what he was doing. And he did it well enough, but not perfectly; otherwise Nicholas would have never spotted him.

Whoever the stranger was, he presented no immediate threat. His stare remained open to interpretation. Perhaps it was just a hobby, something the man pursued when he found himself in a crowded place containing a certain person of interest. If it truly were something else, a hidden intent present behind that scrutinizing stare, Nicholas would decisively meet it head on, parry and reciprocate with lethal force.

Nicholas was thirty-five, with a face that was a cold mask, but from time to time his eyes betrayed his humanness. His enemies knew him as an astute, calculating professional with a glacial gaze. They knew him by reputation—the tales about him, his weapon of choice. But they rarely had the chance to look him in the eyes before he pulled the trigger of his Beretta handgun. If they had, they would have seen that fleeting spark of humanity.

At long last, the train noisily approached the platform. Within minutes Nicholas had handed his ticket to the conductor and boarded the train.

Nicholas moved through the slightly claustrophobic carpeted corridor of the train, passed by the prestigious compartments, the substantially larger and fabulously furnished choice of the upper classes, until he located and stopped in front of his own.

Inside he found two benches positioned on the left and the right-hand sides. Above rested, undisturbed for the time being, rectangular-shaped beds that unfolded from the wall—proffering hopefully a night of deep sleep for the weary traveler before being embedded back into their recesses. The ladder was free floating, deployable when needed, and stored in a corner. A single large window with a miniature folding table underneath completed the picture.

Just when he began to get comfortable, sitting down stretching his legs, a stranger invaded his territory, his personal hibernation chamber. The stranger was an unmistakable beauty in her mid-thirties, with not a single thing bland about her physical features. A real head-turner. An enchantress with artistic curves, and wide eyes that engulfed your every ounce of attention, the type you can always count on to make a dramatic entrance, just as she clearly did now. He even found her perfume to his liking, a healing ointment for his tormented soul. "You look like a scorned female in need of emotional healing."

She let out a short, musical laugh. "Do women get any satisfaction hearing you make false assumptions through these stereotypical sexist male remarks, even though after a while they become monotone?"

"I decided against the usual advances of the... quintessential types."

"Sorry, the *what*... types?"

"Quintessential. Representative of a class, in this case of men. Certain types of men."

She raised her thinnest-blade-of-grass thin eyebrows in puzzlement. "So why not just say that?"

"Well you know men..."

"I do?"

"You aren't afraid to talk to me, so you must."

"I'll take your word for it."

"So these men you know, and possibly don't, are notorious for complicating the simplest of things. Case in point, quintessential."

"So these *quintessential* types, are they men of letters, tutoring pupils in educational institutions? Perhaps they are bricklayers who jot down wisdoms about women on tiny strips of paper, pasting them to one side of the brick and passing them down the chain gang, broadening other male minds. Hmm. All these wise men and their collective wisdom! Their wise teachings should be locatable in any public library, cataloged and made available upon request for further study."

"Might take some time to get the funding and permits for a project of this scale."

"And until then, this information is simply out there? Common knowledge spread by word of mouth? Stored in the minds of all men?"

"You don't want to find yourself stranded without a reference."

She sat across from him on the other vacant bench. "Tell me a bit more about these usual suspects and their methods of approach."

He smiled at her self-assured nature. "The approach of a mild-mannered gentleman, for instance."

"Would a mild-mannered gentleman possess enough boldness to even speak to me?"

"He could, in a very mild sort of way…" That disarming smile brushed his face again.

"And the others?"

"Well, the ferocious approach of... let's say wild animals who use brute force, ones that never take no for an answer, the tall tale-tellers, the braggadocio types..."

"I know the type."

"I bet you do. There are far too many of them."

"And where do you fit into the above selection?"

He retrieved a stainless-steel cigarette case from an inside pocket, selecting the second to last cigarette next to the upside down *lucky one*. A vintage lighter lit this luckless cigarette. "My methodology happens to be quite different. Conceit circles around certain men. Especially those impeccably dressed but obviously obscene men with a singular train of thought. Grotesques with grey hearts, bereft of soul and full of ulterior motives. I reference them only as a guide as to what not to do. I have fervor for knowledge, fidelity for seeking out information. I am not rich

but neither am I a has-been jabbering incoheren-
cies, one of those constantly down-on-their-luck
accursed men. No, I am not like them. I would
love to show you just how. Why don't you accom-
pany me to the dining car this evening."

"We jumped ahead, haven't we?"

"Have we?"

"We have. It's what I would call fast-tracking."

"I thought it was just dinner."

"Dinner between strangers is the pursuance
of romantic possibilities, but we won't ever get
there without you telling me first which category
you fit best."

He raised his hands, palms up in mock surrender. "Guiltless. As I said before I am not like
those men. I am not sure there *is* a category for
me. I get to the point, forgo ornamentation,
remain a realist who often walks along the razor's
edge. Good at intuiting, full of strong convictions,
dependable."

"Dangerous?"

"At times."

"When it's called upon."

"When it's called upon."

"An atypical character, I must say."

"Not your typical chance encounter."

"Hardly."

"Do you approve?"

Her eyes inspected the window, the scurrying sprawled greenery beyond the glass. The whistle sounded as the chugging mechanical beast approached a crossing. "Remains to be seen. I do like the idea of getting straight to the point and skipping falseness, insufferable boredom, the explosive stupefying anger whenever the more swinish type of suitor cannot have their way. My husband was very good at that triplicate."

"*Was.* Deceased?"

"Abandoned. But do spare me the congratulations on my newfound freedom. Do you know why?"

"Because it took such a long time for this annulment to transpire."

"Too long."

"Too long for you to have forgotten who you once were? Outside the abused domesticated housewife who forfeited her rights, her freedom, her previous life."

"It could come back."

"Let's hope sooner than later."

"Why don't we try tonight over that dinner you proposed. See if we can rekindle the fire, even if it is just a flamelet." She gave him a bittersweet smile.

He matched her smile with a more reassuring one. "Accepted."

"I just want you to know he wasn't all bad. I hope I don't sound incurably wrathful about my marriage."

"Don't. I do not like flip-floppers. Nothing you could have done would equal the amount of hurt he inflicted. I could stand here and try to do the same for my younger brother, blame myself, defend his actions, but he was always in control, responsible for himself, for his degenerate ways, his gambling addiction, constantly being in debt with loan sharks and living of all places in Las Vegas."

"Those strike me as different vices."

"Two degenerates sharing one umbrella."

"You don't let go easily, do you?"

"I never let go."

"So, I never stood a chance of declining your dinner invitation in the first place?"

"Even if you had that option, would you want to?"

"I suppose not. Anything is better than the past. Any glimmer of hope. If my father taught me one lesson, that was to always keep my head up whenever something bad happened. To remember that something better would arise as long as I acknowledged the truth. The ability to keep moving forward."

"Now you are on the move."

"We both are."

"You know, it's somewhat of a rarity to have unexpectedly found myself in the presence of a charming..." he paused for a word, found it, "...*coquettish* countess. I suppose I am not a big believer in coincidental meetings, especially aboard a moving train in a cabin I reserved beforehand selfishly all to myself."

"Calling me a *countess* might be an exaggeration. *Charming*, most definitely. *Coquettish* solely depends on the quality and quantity of wine at dinner."

"Sounds divine. I could not have asked for more. A splendid opportunity to spend some quality time with the woman I am going to sleep with..." Nicholas let this phrase linger in the air before uttering its completion, "...in the same compartment."

"Before I fail to recall it at a later date, a friend of yours was leaving you a note under the door while I was inside surveying the premises, having just bribed the conductor to let me occupy it with you for the sheer experience of being in a first-class compartment. Mind you, I didn't get a very good look at him, he kept his face covered with a handkerchief, but he asked me to give you this." She handed Nicholas a folded note.

Inside, written in longhand, were five words: "I KNOW WHO YOU ARE."

Later in the day, our anti-hero and his nameless companion, the charming coquettish countess, traversed along to the dining car, captivated by the guests liberally enjoying themselves.

A whirlpool of activity greeted them there:

The stentorian voices of scurrying waiters, clattering cutlery; scrapping of the constantly moving chairs; patient waiters reminding one of timeless towering Greek statues permanently perched over the shoulders of certain capricious personages vacillating between choices of wine; the constant rotational changing of decimated white tablecloths spotted with insignias of satiety, and everywhere vivacious personalities filling the dining car with resounding laughter.

One sacrilegist decided not to join in the festivities. An oddity. The dullest sort of fellow, one who most likely leads a solitary life, the silent type, detached from the rest of the world, here sitting by himself engrossed in his dinner. A pitiable creature at first sight, with a sallow face and asymmetrical lips.

Nicholas and his dinner guest passed him on the way to their table at the very end of the dining car, close to the wheels, and as such forcing them to lean in closer to be heard.

Once seated and with their order placed, the charming coquettish countess gave Nicholas her best conversation-starter smile. When this subtlety escaped him, she leaned in even closer, taking matters into her own hands, "What should we talk about?"

"What do people generally talk about?"

"They ask questions. Questions that help them leaf through a person."

"To check for suitability?"

"Likeness of mind."

"Suitability."

"Suitability."

17

"They end up foraging."

"For details."

"To help with their understanding of the other."

"Exactly."

"Exhumation of the human soul."

"Well, it doesn't have to be that deep."

"Doesn't it? Deep conversations are the only ones worth having."

"Why do you find short conversations so unendurable?"

"Because they are short."

"Don't they add up to the same result?"

"But much too late. Some like precision, decisiveness. Some slowness, mundanity. Some can afford to take their time, others can't." His face matched the language, sternness of chosen words.

"It's an issue with time for you then."

"Yes."

"With waiting."

"Very much so. I am not the waiting type."

"That you aren't."

"But some are."

She gave him a hurt look, feeling singled out. "If you are talking about me, I'd say I am somewhat in the middle. I was used to waiting when I was a married woman. I waited for an awfully long time. And then I did not want to wait any longer. But I also did not want to rid myself completely of waiting in my life, so I decided to practice what you could call the fifty-fifty principle."

"I didn't mean you, just so you know."

She exhaled with relief. "Oh. I thought you did mean me."

"No, no. I meant the gentleman sitting two tables up from us. Medium height, far from lustrous hair, receding in fact, unshaven, slightly overweight if there ever is such a thing as slight. His clothes are up-to-date, modern, fashionable, but wrinkled. His dinner is entirely predictable, bland."

She turned her head a little, shifted her eyes to the gentleman. "You really have him pegged.

I appreciate how you dismantled him using your power of observation, I just don't understand why."

"It's simple. His actions are premeditative. He wants us to think he's having a straightforward dinner, sitting alone minding his own business."

"But he isn't."

"No. He certainly isn't."

She paused. "What is he doing then?"

"He is observing. Listening."

"I don't see the big deal. He is alone. He is lonely. So what if he looks around a bit?"

"He's looked in only one direction with any real interest, aside from his feigned interest in his dinner. In ours. At us."

"Well so much for a conventional conversation."

"Predictability pervades most conversations. Aren't you tired of predictability?"

"Well put. I suppose I am."

"One must strive to be uninhibited, anomalous,

completely original in the presence of someone as lovely as you." She blushed, darting her sparkling eyes downward. "You are good." She paused, slightly uncomfortable. "That man wasn't really watching us, was he?"

"No, of course not. Just me. But do not worry, he is most likely a poorly miser with miserly fixations such as voyeurism. He likes to drop in on other people's good time. Let him get an eyeful."

"And an earful."

In their shared compartment, Nicholas watched the woman sleep. Complaining of migraine pain, she retired early, swallowed a capsule and closed her eyelids, waiting for the calmative effect to take place, not wanting to face any more reality.

He had felt tired as well, and favored the idea of joining her in hibernation. But now he was having too much trouble falling asleep, tossing and turning in his bed.

Over the course of his lifetime, Nicholas had

never considered himself lucky or blessed with remarkable gifts. His skills were painstakingly accumulated, chiseled in solitary practice as part of his ascetic lifestyle, unaided by others whose teachings he abhorred. He abstained from the usualness of things, fully entrusting himself to the doctrine of self-reliance and perfecting those skills over many years.

The one noteworthy advantage he had over others was his acute hearing. But this was both a blessing and curse, as his ears were hellbent on picking up everything, constantly alerting him, bringing to the forefront even the most meritless noises.

After an hour of trying to sleep, Nicholas, no longer even groggy, sat up in bed. His eyes spun about the room, scrutinizing, probing, until he found himself focusing on the cabin's door. He strained his eyes, refocused his vision. Something on the other side was blocking the streak of light between the door and the floor. The width of the intruder's shadow suggested a single person.

And while the strange figure had not intruded, he was probably intending to, poised and listening, waiting for the right moment to strike. Nicholas reached under his pillow and retrieved his loaded, suppressed Beretta—the safety already off so as not to make any noise. Some would call this rush dizzying. But for him, there was only a feeling akin to oceanic calmness. This was second nature. Nicholas tightened his grip on the handle, the gun an open invitation for the intruder to step inside.

However, the knock announcing this lurker's presence never sounded. The door handle never turned. A lockpick never got inserted to manipulate the lock. Was it timidity? Hesitancy? Second thoughts? Even over the clatter of the train, Nicholas heard a distinct rustling as another poison pen letter slid underneath the door. More insinuations, character defamation, perhaps a request for the almighty dollar.

The real truth was certainly ascertainable. Nicholas firmly believed in logical deduction, the discoverable nature of even the most complex problems. There was a perfectly sound justification for this interloper's actions, the driving force, the motivational factor behind their criss-crossing paths aboard this train. Nicholas would figure it all out in his spare time once he did away with the burdensome aspect of the murder.

He moved quickly, quietly unlocking and opening the door, cautiously stepping over the note on the floor, just in time to catch sight of the fleeing quarry. The straight-line layout of the passenger car certainly simplified matters. Nicholas smiled, a secret smile implying a private joke: in his need to flee, the stranger forgot the cardinal rule of reconnaissance—look behind you. Except for prey and predator, as Nicholas dubbed them in his mind, the corridor was empty. The stranger carelessly kept propelling forward, traversing the tight passageway, still never bothering to look back, aiming for the connecting doors between the cars. With his sole focus forward and zero visibility behind, the stranger made for an easy target.

Nicholas picked up pace, moving in for the kill.

He shortened the distance, positioning himself directly behind his oblivious victim fully immersed with the task at hand of trying to open the connecting door.

Nicholas pounced, smothering the man's mouth, not wanting to hear any exhortations for life, then raised his gun, tightly gripped by his other hand, and struck down hard, liberating his victim of his consciousness before promptly extracting the stranger's limp body back with him, averting any suspicion along the way through pretense: A pair of boozed comrades supporting one another with linked arms, both returning to their respective cabins.

He kept up the charade until he reached his compartment. Straining slightly, supporting the stranger's weight, he opened the door, noting satisfactorily nothing had changed in his absence. The compartment remained the epicenter of dead silence, with no detectable stirrings.

Nicholas lowered the body, dragged it inside far enough to clear it of the door's path, then closed the door gingerly with his outstretched foot. His eyes never left the sleeping beauty's face in her berth as the lock *clicked* into place. He waited but did not spot any facial twitching or notice any changes in her breathing.

This made him smile, having dodged the undesirable. Nicholas took hold of the stranger once more, dragging his unconscious body toward the window, a short distance in very tight quarters, until his heel bumped against a solid surface, feeling the materialized back wall with one hand.

Nicholas stood up at full height. A momentary pause. The much-needed break from all the physical effort. He stood there, motionless except for his eyes. Eyes that roamed. Eyes that moved along the compartment until they met another set, the woman's, now widely opened, full of alertness.

She slowly sat up, reaching for her glasses. The situation clearly was an ungraspable one for her.

Nicholas gripped her unsteady hand, stopping her from putting on her glasses. He manipulated her arm downward, setting it on her lap, met there eagerly by her other slightly trembling hand—now an even set of two, trembling together, positioned in a payer position around her spectacles. Nicholas then placed his palm over her eyes, gently shutting her eyelids.

Through the crevices formed by his splayed fingers, she fought hard to focus, fought against her farsighted vision, battling the blurriness, and briefly improving the distortion enough to witness the veil of darkness suddenly lifted, and the compartment filled with a bright torchlight flame.

Unmistakable to a woman whose husband hunted as a pastime, her ears knew the ever-eerie sound of the bullet leaving the chamber, quelled by the silencer. About the same time, she smelled the rush of hot air that resembled sulfur.

While many would have taken a look just

then to satisfy their curiosity, their inquiry con-
firming or denying the conclusions arrived at, she
saw this as a terrible mistake which would only
lead to certain death.

Her death.

So, she remained still, remained seated, stat-
uesque, even with Nicholas bustling about her.
She could not pinpoint his every movement, but
she could tell he had his hands full moving around
the compartment altogether unsuitable for three
people. That is why she supposed he was remov-
ing the third party...

She felt nauseous inside, holding back a hys-
teric outburst, her organs squirming and refusing
to stay put. A living being, breathing the same air,
cut down mere seconds ago...

Slight noises reached her, and then a breeze
that started to sanitize the stagnant, sulfuric
air. Nicholas had opened the window. How else
would one get rid of a body in here? This moving cramped catacomb. He was now bent over the
body, lifting it, the dead dangling arms reminding

her of a drowned man fished from a river. And out that body went, discarded like refuse, scattered from the window like ashes—abandoned to decay in the wilderness.

She could not help to wonder about the view outside. Her thoughts, unfortunately, could not reach a consensus. In one version she saw the clear window, outside of which farmland greeted her, constant and uneventful. The houses looked similar, with rotting wood, peeling paint, barns housing farm stock, blossoming flowers, and an overall prolonged stillness except for the lightly wavering grass.

In the second version, the blood spatter has smudged the window. Outside, the land is barren, with something under the surface giving it movement, a bubbling beneath causing earthly tremors, draining and unnerving her, peeling and stripping away, a concocted nightmare cannibalizing her, trying to satiate its appetite for succulent humanity.

After he disposed of the body, he came over

and held her under a wool woven blanket. His touch was oppressive and singeing to her skin. Her mind raced feverishly.

Nicholas awoke to the feeling that something was not how it should have been. The scene, his present reality modified, his design tempered with. Sunlight spilt through the window and the blanket lay flat against the bed. The train had stopped, and he was all alone. An occurrence he had not anticipated had taken place in the middle of the night while he watchfully kept his eye on her resting body.

He must have closed his eyes, entering deep sleep, dreaming for once, an absurdist dream ripped right from the pages of a fantasist's notebook. In the dream Nicholas was choking the murdered man. The man kept rasping, gulping for air, trying to express himself in a garbled language, a communication system consisting entirely of guttural noises a gutted animal might make.

30

Her disappearance was unmistakably a hindrance. He had to attend to the situation immediately, and he was already behind. Losing time where it counts most always puts you in an inferior position. But he would find her and make her understand. Persuade her with pleasant words or deaden the hollow pain she must feel inside right now; the type of pain that circulates continuously while always returning to the heart to inflict more hurt.

Nicholas holstered his gun, left the cabin and with great concentration descended the locomotive to the brightly-lit sidewalk, slightly past the train station. The train must have just perched here, the screeching halt intrusively cutting through the fabric of his slumber. Thankfully this happened to be the penultimate stop before his own.

He head-hunted for her along the paved paths illuminated by the sun's brilliance, until he collided with a current of people, all in a rush, blurred faces in fast-motion heading toward their different destinations. He marvelled at the militant synchronicity of their steps. Disoriented now, unsure of his destination, fearing this marching battalion might single him out, he infused himself with them, surrendering himself to the mob, not wanting to be the one who stopped.

Once he synchronized himself, figured out the rhythm of the crowd, he moved with gracefulness. His gaze passed over concrete businesses, and brick residential homes, moving and parked cars, signs signaling direction and enforcing rules, more moving and stationary foot traffic, and air polluting trucks and buses all crammed into one area of a busy bustling city. And just when surrender seemed imminent, he found himself staring at a picturesque sight, one he nearly missed:

A park filled with devotees to the sun, a divine and paradisiacal place, full of blossoming flowers and immeasurable greenery trampled underneath the feet of happily screaming children chasing one another and passing the bench where she sat deep in thought.

She stared ahead with unbroken concentration, the sun's curative properties wholly lost on her. With a furrowed forehead and a face reflecting nothing but fear and worry, she emitted none of her usual radiance. She was alone on the bench, as if all the others were keeping a certain distance, sensing her wanting to be alone.

Nichols sat down next to her. She never acknowledged him, kept staring hypnotically ahead. He looked around, remaining calm and estimating the value or risks.

They happened to be in a very popular part of the park. The situation did not greatly improve when Nicholas noticed two constables speaking in the dialect of the region, positioned some distance away, but a bit too close for comfort.

"You are distraught, that's understandable. Don't you think I understand? I am wholeheartedly on your side."

"You are bereft of conscience."

"You think less of me now?"

A look of incredulity passed over her face.

"You murdered a man."

He eyed the constables, said nothing.

"And for what?" she said. "Why?"

"Self preservation. As absurd as this notion is, I was not willing to forfeit my own life. I could sit here and attempt to justify my actions, attempt to lessen the impact. But we both know I won't."

Her hand whitely clenched the edge of the bench. "Are you going to murder me now?"

"I don't have to. Mum's the word, right?"

"How can I live with myself?"

"The same way you lived with yourself when you became stuck in a loveless marriage. Bear through it. That's all any strong woman can do."

"Did you actually feel nothing? Not an ounce of pity? You could have spared him. Tied him up. He wasn't a threat to you then, lying on the floor comatose, defenseless."

He looked over, looked away. "It's almost impossible to stop once you start."

"But you didn't even try."

A quick nod. "That I did not."

"You know… I think you did feel something. You felt empowerment, releasing all that hatred you felt as a child—jealousy, parental love distributed unequally between you and your brother. Acceptance cannot be gained with a pistol, and neither can love."

"Freudian assumptions aside, my childhood was a happy one. Swell. Uneventful."

"And yet look at you now… A journeying Satan."

"And here I thought you might refer to my voyage as a spiritual pilgrimage!"

"More like the path of a disease. Pestilence dead set on wiping out humanity."

He snickered. "Such archaic concepts. Biblical. Reeks of righteousness. Sadly, it just doesn't work in this rotting world that has disowned all higher power."

"Have you noticed, that as much as you try to anticipate your opponent's next move, they still once in a while find a way to surprise you?"

"I wouldn't do that if I were you. I would not have given it thought to begin with, but now that you clearly have, make sure you do everything in your power not to give it another. As much as I have enjoyed our conversational interlude, I want to remind you that I do not feel languid, nor have my body or mind atrophied sitting on this bench. And you would be greatly mistaken if you think I have not spotted those constables to our right, entranced in a very lively conversation, it seems. Whatever is being discussed, it must be utterly enthralling for these two public servants to have completely forgotten about patrolling, completely forgotten about being the watchmen of the street and that in their absence, or in absence of their complete attention, there might be a rise in all sorts of criminal activities, a direct correlation if you will. Preoccupation with a subject is great; complete immersion is extremely dangerous."

"How did you describe yourself when we first met? Dangerous at times, if I remember correctly. Isn't that so? Perhaps so am I. Perhaps I should get up and stretch my legs."

"I do believe this would be a fatal mistake. A clear case of threadbare logic."

She turned to him, fully facing him, smiling crazily at her potential executioner. "So, you *are* going to kill me."

"If you force my hand."

"I wouldn't be able to live with myself if I didn't try to stop you."

"Ah, that prickling sense of duty. The need to right a wrong and administer justice. To rush to those two constables and pronounce distinctly, without delay, that right behind you sitting on this very bench is the scourge of society—a man who murders. And who could blame you? You are blameless. These emotions are not counterfeit. You have an obligation. To yourself. The world at large. The society you are a part of. It all has that ring of trueness to it. Hell, it's downright inspirational really, I'll give you that." He shrugged. "The sad reality is that you wouldn't even have the time to stand up."

"Do you think that scares me?"

"It should. But I know it does not. Not when it's just you and your sense of justice."

"You know me well."

"I do. I even know things that you tried to keep away from me. For example, do you know what the word 'anthesis' means? It's of Greek origin, roughly defined as, 'to blossom,' which is something your unborn child cannot do, blossom that is, if it's short-life is further shortened by an irretrievably bad decision made by its law-abiding mother."

She let out an unnatural fit of laughter, momentarily drawing the attention of the two constables.

"I will only warn you once more. There will not be any warnings after that." Nicholas slid his hand inside his jacket pretending to search for something in the breast pocket, unholstered his gun and hid it amid a great many pages of a discarded newspaper next to him. "When I think about the first time we met, what stood out for me the most was your smell. I could really smell your perfume, the fragrance of perspiration left behind on the back of your neck, and, of course, the fragrant smell of your unborn child. We have my increased nasal sensitivity to thank for a more level playing field. It seems we both have something important to lose. I just hope you make the right decision."

If I may interject, this remarkable story will not have a conventional ending. The ending splinters into a pair of distinct possibilities:

In his version, Nicholas succeeds in convincing her. A truly triumphant moment. He has no doubts about her ability to keep a secret. He has made his point, and she has understood everything. She even agrees with him, admitting she was rash and over-zealous in her pursuance of justice.

He watches the children playing, digging trenches in the sandbox. Allying themselves against a common enemy. The enemy is unseen, but its presence is felt and they continue to dig at a more frenetic pace, fortifying their position. These are not your ordinary children, this is a unit, each member persnickety about completion of their assigned task. Their insularity on full display. Neutralization of the foreign enemy to ensure their country's survival. Their structure would not crumble, the unit would not cower. This trench would be a resting place to some of them, those whose prayers will go unanswered. The dignified death of a true soldier. A befitting death. The big one might have been over and forgotten by the world, but these smaller and equally personal wars were still being waged.

Nicholas extricates himself before the first shot rings out, the air thick with threat. They are surrounded from all sides. He knows the outcome facing those soldiers, those condemned men with darting, sunken eyes.

His own eyes dart, as if anticipating something. Seconds later, a car—elegant, enormous,

colored black after a tar explosion—comes to a
halt and stations itself near the exit to the park.

Nicholas stands, commemorates their chance
encounter with a firmly planted kiss on the
lips, and enters the automobile's familiar leath-
er-bound interior with ease. His occupancy rean-
imates the vehicle, tailpipe discharges wrath as
the passenger side window slowly rolls down. It is
absurd to see the sarcastic, almost sneering smile,
to hear his undignified laugh, but it is there in the
richness of his handsome, unaffected face. The
window rolls back up, the automobile flies forward and disappears.

In her version: She stood up.

ABOUT THE AUTHOR

A native of Kyiv, Ukraine, but living in Canada since the age of eleven, Nick Voro discovered literature at an early age, never quite mustering the ability to put an excellent book down. A recent graduate of the Toronto Film School, Nick divides his time between being a full-time parent and a full-time author.

His debut work, *Conversational Therapy: Stories and Plays*, has recently sold over 200 copies and is part of the library system (United States, Canada, New Zealand, Australia and Scotland).

Lee D. Thompson, an editor and writer from Moncton, New Brunswick, Canada, edited this short story. His books include: a novel in [xxx] dreams from Broken Jaw Press, Mouth Human Must Die from Frog Hollow Press and Apastoral: A Mistopia from Corona/Samizdat. His short fiction has been published in many anthologies, including Random House's Victory Meat, New Fiction from Atlantic Canada and Vagrant Press's The Vagrant Revue of New Fiction. He is the winner of the David Adams Richards Prize (2018) and New Brunswick Book Award (2022). He is the publisher of Galleon Books.